VISIONS

Red Cow by Leonora Carrington.

VISIONS

Stories About Women Artists

Mary Cassatt · Betye Saar

Leonora Carrington · Mary Frank

LESLIE SILLS

Albert Whitman & Company   Morton Grove, Illinois

For Bob

I want to thank the people at Albert Whitman—Kathy Tucker, Joe Boyd, Ann Fay, and Abby Levine—for their steadfast support of me and this project. I also appreciate the cooperation and assistance of artists Betye Saar and Mary Frank and galleries Coe Kerr, Brewster, and Zabriskie. I thank Rebecca and Justin Elswit for their feedback on my text and picture selection. Thanks to Money for Women/The Barbara Deming Memorial Fund, Inc., for sisterly and financial support. I also want to note that this book could not have been written without the research and writing of many art scholars, more than I can name here. Hayden Herrera's work on Mary Frank was pivotal. Nancy Mowll Mathews' writings on Mary Cassatt; Whitney Chadwick's and Janet Kaplan's on surrealist women artists; and Gloria Feman Orenstein's and Dr. Salomón Grimberg's on Leonora Carrington all contributed immensely. Dr. Grimberg's ideas, encouragement, and continual empathy, in fact, have been inspirational. Lastly, my husband, Robert Oresick, and son, Eric, have been editors supreme!

Library of Congress Cataloging-in-Publication Data

Sills. Leslie.
   Visions : stories about women artists / Leslie Sills.
     p. cm.
   Summary: Presents the lives and works of four pioneering women artists: Mary Cassatt, Leonora Carrington, Betye Saar, and Mary Frank.
   ISBN 0-8075-8491-6
   1. Women artists—Biography—Juvenile literature. [1. Women artists. 2. Artists.] I. Title.
N42.S56 1993
709' .2'2—dc20
[B]   92-32909
                                    CIP
                                     AC

CURR
N
42
.S56
1993

VISIONS
Stories About Women Artists

Mary Cassatt · Betye Saar
Leonora Carrington · Mary Frank

LESLIE SILLS

Albert Whitman & Company   Morton Grove, Illinois

For Bob

I want to thank the people at Albert Whitman—Kathy Tucker, Joe Boyd, Ann Fay, and Abby Levine—for their steadfast support of me and this project. I also appreciate the cooperation and assistance of artists Betye Saar and Mary Frank and galleries Coe Kerr, Brewster, and Zabriskie. I thank Rebecca and Justin Elswit for their feedback on my text and picture selection. Thanks to Money for Women/The Barbara Deming Memorial Fund, Inc., for sisterly and financial support. I also want to note that this book could not have been written without the research and writing of many art scholars, more than I can name here. Hayden Herrera's work on Mary Frank was pivotal. Nancy Mowll Mathews' writings on Mary Cassatt; Whitney Chadwick's and Janet Kaplan's on surrealist women artists; and Gloria Feman Orenstein's and Dr. Salomón Grimberg's on Leonora Carrington all contributed immensely. Dr. Grimberg's ideas, encouragement, and continual empathy, in fact, have been inspirational. Lastly, my husband, Robert Oresick, and son, Eric, have been editors supreme!

Library of Congress Cataloging-in-Publication Data

Sills. Leslie.
   Visions : stories about women artists / Leslie Sills.
      p.   cm.
   Summary: Presents the lives and works of four pioneering women artists: Mary Cassatt, Leonora Carrington, Betye Saar, and Mary Frank.
   ISBN 0-8075-8491-6
   1. Women artists—Biography—Juvenile literature. [1. Women artists. 2. Artists.] I. Title.
N42.S56 1993
709' .2'2—dc20
[B]   92-32909
                                                           CIP
                                                            AC

Text © 1993 by Leslie Sills.
Cover and interior design by Karen Yops.
Published in 1993 by Albert Whitman & Company,
6340 Oakton St., Morton Grove, IL 60053-2723.
Printed in U.S.A. All rights reserved.

10 9 8 7 6 5 4 3 2 1

CONTENTS

Mary Cassatt

Detail from engraving showing Mary Cassatt with her brothers Robbie and Gardner, 1854.

When Mary Stevenson Cassatt was a little girl, looking at art was an important part of her family life. Yet no one in her family had ever been an artist. Her sister, Lydia, and three brothers, Alexander, Gardner, and Robbie, were all drawn to more practical pursuits such as sewing, physics, and math. Mary, the next-to-youngest child, wanted to do something different. Perhaps she sensed that being an artist was how she could win her family's respect and establish *her* place in the world.

Mary was born on May 22, 1844, in Allegheny City, Pennsylvania, to Katherine and Robert Cassatt. As a child, she was called "May" by her mother and "Mame" by her father. She was attractive, tall and slender, yet not as pretty as she thought her father wished.

Her energy was unusual. Her oldest brother, Alexander, once said that she was always ready for any activity, even horseback riding in bad weather. He also recalled that she had a "quick temper." They would frequently quarrel but soon make up.

Throughout her life, Mary had strong opinions about almost everything and didn't hesitate to express them.

Mary's mother, Katherine, was particularly well educated for an American woman in the nineteenth century. She knew a lot about the arts, literature, and world events. She had studied with a European-educated teacher and spoke fluent French.

Mary's father, Robert, was a successful banker and, for a time, the mayor of Allegheny City. When Mary was seven years old, he hired an artist to paint a portrait of Mary's three brothers. While Mary might have liked to be in the painting, too, she was fascinated watching the entire process. It was her first experience meeting an artist.

A few months later, the Cassatt family moved to Paris, France. Robert thought Europe a good place for his children to learn, and it was. Mary learned to speak French and often visited one of the world's best art museums, the Louvre. She loved the work of the "old masters," famous painters from the past such as Leonardo da Vinci, Titian, and Rembrandt. She also loved watching art students copying paintings, then a popular way to learn how to paint.

Although all were happy, Mary's father decided that living in Germany, where schools emphasized mathematics and science, would encourage Alexander's talents. They moved to Heidelberg and then Darmstadt, only to face a tragedy. Mary's brother Robbie, who had been seriously ill with a knee-joint disease, died at the age of twelve. The grief-stricken Cassatts now decided to return home to Pennsylvania.

Mary was eleven that year. By her sixteenth birthday, she had decided to become an artist. She didn't want to be an amateur artist like many young girls. She planned to be a professional, to make art her life's work. In fact, she told a friend, she was going to paint better than the old masters!

From 1860 to 1862, Mary studied at the Pennsylvania Academy of the Fine Arts in a program that emphasized drawing of the human body. She learned a great deal in her classes, but there were not many good paintings to study in the Academy's collection or even in any American museums. What Mary really wanted to do was to return to Europe to study painting seriously. She believed that the only way to learn to be an artist was to study and copy the work of the old masters.

When Mary told her parents of her goals, her father reportedly said, "I would almost rather see you dead!" Yet Mary was determined. She argued with her parents until they agreed. As a compromise,

Mary's mother traveled with her and helped her get settled. Mary was then twenty-two.

After arriving in Paris, Mary arranged to paint in two private studios with Charles Chaplin and Jean-Léon Gérôme. Both these artists were successful, showing their work every year in the Paris Salon.

The annual Salon exhibition was the most important event in an artist's career. Not only would a painting accepted for the exhibit be seen and sold, but one's future success would practically be ensured. To be accepted into the Salon, however, meant one's work was judged by a group of men, called a jury, who had narrow ideas about what was good or bad art. These judges, or jurors, preferred paintings about myths, history, or literature. They thought modern life was a distasteful subject for art. They liked to see characters in art idealized, painted to look like heroes or gods rather than ordinary people. They thought the paint should be dark, with all the colors blended. The texture should be smooth, glossy, and polished like the work of the old masters.

In spite of Mary's love for the old masters, she came to realize that being a good artist meant finding her own style. She and her painting friend Eliza Haldeman left their teachers to copy pictures

Mary Cassatt, about 1872.

in the Louvre and paint in the countryside. Often they hired local people to dress in costumes and pose for them. Sometimes they studied with other teachers.

During this time, in the 1860s, the French art world was changing. Two artists, Gustave Courbet and Edouard Manet, began a rebellion, challenging the control of the Salon. Both of these men painted scenes of modern life and refused to paint people in an idealized way. Courbet liked to paint in a loose, free manner. He loved the paint as much as his subject and sometimes worked with his fingers instead of a brush. Manet also painted freely and especially enjoyed using highly contrasting colors. One critic said that his coloring "stabs the eyes like a steel saw."

Many critics as well as the general public were shocked by the work of Courbet and Manet. Perhaps Mary did not know what to think at first. She did understand, however, their need to be independent, to paint without restrictions. Just the same, she wanted to be recognized by the Salon.

In the spring of 1868, her wish came true. Her painting *A Mandolin Player* was accepted and even displayed in a place of honor. It shows a peasant girl in costume, holding a mandolin and thoughtfully looking to one side. Except for a soft light on the girl, the entire painting is dark, in the manner preferred by the Salon jurors.

Mary was thrilled to have her painting accepted. When a second one was also accepted, in 1870, she felt more like a real artist than a student. In the summer of 1870, however, the Franco-Prussian (French and German) War broke out and, once again, Mary had to return to America.

Mary was miserable! She wrote to a friend, "I cannot tell you what I suffer from the want of seeing a good picture." Now living in a small town, Hollidaysburg, Pennsylvania, Mary was unable to find models or supplies. Her father also decided he

A Mandolin Player, about 1868.

no longer wanted to support her career financially. When Mary tried to sell her work in New York City, she was unsuccessful. Paintings that she tried to sell in Chicago were destroyed in the Great Chicago Fire of 1871.

Still, Mary was not discouraged. She found a way to return to Europe. A Catholic bishop from Pittsburgh asked her to copy two paintings in Parma, Italy, by a sixteenth-century Italian Renaissance painter named Correggio. Mary was delighted.

She thought Correggio "perhaps the greatest painter that ever lived." He made flesh look real and captured the tender communication between a mother and child. His work influenced Mary years later, when she painted mothers with their children.

After having a third painting accepted by the Salon, Mary traveled for two years, studying and copying the old masters as well as working on her own painting. She pushed herself to see and do as much as possible. Sometimes she climbed tall ladders to look at art in cold, dark churches. She went to Spain alone, knowing no one and not speaking the language. She sometimes suffered from stomach pains but did not let them stop her. Her passion for art fueled her. "Oh dear," she wrote, "to think that there is no one I can shriek to, beautiful! lovely, oh! painting what ar'nt you."

Studying so many paintings helped Mary discover what she wanted to accomplish. She wrote about one of her paintings, "I know that it is heavy, but how to get a thing solid and yet keep it easy." Her goal was to create realistic figures that appeared effortlessly painted.

In 1873, Mary had a fourth acceptance by the Salon, *Torrero and Young Girl.* Despite her artistic successes, she was growing more and more critical of the Salon's standards. She, in fact, lost friends over her strong views. A once-close painting friend wrote about Mary, saying she "is entirely too slashing." Mary felt she had good reason. A painting she had sent to the Salon was rejected, she thought, just because of its bright colors. When she darkened the background and resubmitted it the following year, it was accepted.

Meanwhile, in 1873, a group of artists had formed who shared Mary's disgust with the Salon. In 1874, they held their own exhibition. While each artist had his or her own style, they were united by common concerns. They all strongly disapproved of the jury system and believed that artists should be free to paint as they wish. They wanted to portray modern life, not the past. They thought that art should be about real things, not imaginary ones. However, they didn't want to record life in an impersonal way. They wanted to look closely and then paint what they, as individuals, saw and felt.

Influenced by the newly invented camera, these artists sought to capture the fleeting quality of life. To make their work seem spontaneous, they often drew "from life" rather than from a model posed in a studio. Light and bright color were especially important to them. They were sensitive to how light changes color, how bright morning light, for example, can make something look whiter, while sunset will add a yellowish cast.

Maternal Caress (about 1896) shows the love between a mother and child.

The way in which they applied paint was also different. To catch the changing effects of light and the liveliness of color, they put down patches of color next to each other, creating a mosaic effect. Looking at so many colors up close, it is hard to make sense of the subject. At a distance, however, the colors blend and the forms become clear.

Many people could not get used to this new art. One newspaper critic, who despised the work,

mockingly called the group the Impressionists, after the painting *Impression: Sunrise* by Claude Monet, a member of the group. This name caught on. Today Impressionists are considered important contributors to the history of art.

When one of the painters, Edgar Degas, asked Mary to join them, she accepted joyfully. Later she said, "At last I could work with complete independence without concerning myself with the eventual judgment of a jury. I already knew who were my masters. I admired Manet, Courbet, and Degas. I hated conventional art. I began to live."

Mary had seen Degas' pastels, drawings made from colored chalks, in a gallery window before she had met him. His bold compositions and lifelike figures made such a strong impression on her that many years later she recalled, "I used to go and flatten my nose against that window and absorb all I could of his art. It changed my life. I saw art then as I wanted to see it."

Degas became Mary's close friend. They were both passionate about art and believed in the importance of drawing. They enjoyed going to museums together as well as to restaurants and horse races. Sometimes Degas gave Mary gifts, among them a dog and a poem he wrote about her pet parrot. They were, however, fiercely opinionated people. Occasionally they argued so intensely that they wouldn't see one another for weeks. Nevertheless, their friendship lasted for forty years.

From time to time, Degas asked Mary to be his model. In a print, *Mary Cassatt at the Louvre,* he captured her tall, elegant style. He portrayed her from the back because he loved mystery and enjoyed doing things in unexpected ways.

In 1877, Mary's mother, father, and sister,

Mary Cassatt at the Louvre (1885) by Edgar Degas.

Lydia, moved to Paris to live with her permanently. Lydia was her almost constant companion. On vacations, her brothers' families would visit, as well. While family responsibilities took time away from Mary's work, she was able to complete eleven new paintings for the Impressionist exhibition of 1879. Mary's father was so proud of her that he boasted, "She is now known to the Art world as well as to the general public in such a way as not to be forgotten again so long as she continues to paint!"

In *At the Theatre,* a pastel drawing, the Impressionist style is clear. Mary's lines are broken and quick. Reflected in a mirror, her model shimmers with light. Her face and shoulders have many colors. Mary, like the other Impressionists, did not assume what color something was. Carefully observing, she saw orange and red, blue and green, even charcoal in her model's skin.

Lydia at a Tapestry Loom also shows how Mary's work developed. Here Lydia is captured in a private moment, weaving at her loom. She is not posed like the models of Mary's earlier paintings. In the Impressionist style, Mary worked spontaneously with loose, sketchy brushstrokes. Sunlight shines through the white curtains, bathing Lydia in brightness. Only her face is painted distinctly. It shows the intensity she feels at work. This painting

At the Theatre, about 1879.

celebrates Lydia's skill as a craftswoman and expresses Mary's love for her sister.

Although Mary's work had matured and was now selling, her life began to fill with difficulties.

Lydia at a Tapestry Loom, about 1881.

In 1882, her beloved sister, Lydia, died of a kidney ailment, leaving Mary too sad to paint for more than six months. Then, the Impressionists had begun to argue so bitterly over membership that gradually they dissolved as a group. Mary was also concerned with the well being of her mother, whose health deteriorated after Lydia's death. Mary traveled with her to Spain. There the warmer climate helped them both feel better.

When they returned, Mary's work changed again. She was still an Impressionist in her belief in artistic freedom and her concern for realistically showing modern life. Sometimes she even deliberately chose homely models. However, she began to simplify her approach, to work in a more controlled way. She included only enough lines to convey form and express emotion. At the end of the 1880s, Mary made prints which show this new way of working.

The Map (or *The Lesson*) is an example of a printmaking technique called drypoint. Here two young girls, perhaps close friends or sisters, are sitting at a table studying what could be a map. While this picture looks like a simple drawing, it is actually composed of hundreds of tiny interwoven lines. These lines are made by scratching with a sharp needle on a sheet of copper, called a plate. The scratches are really grooves that hold ink. After being inked, the plate is pressed onto a piece of paper so that a reverse impression of the drawing is picked up. Mary liked making drypoints, in particular, because they challenged her ability to draw. There can be no erasing. "One can't cheat," she said.

The Map (or The Lesson), 1889.

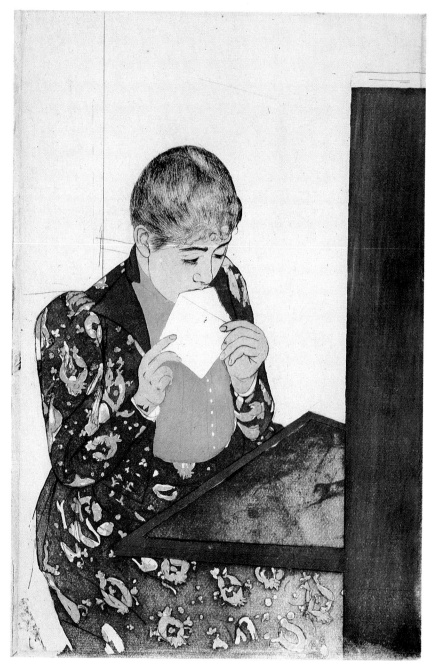

The Letter, about 1891.

Mary also did an important series of colored prints inspired by an exhibition of Japanese woodblock prints. Her prints involved drypoint and several other demanding printmaking processes. They are so complicated yet so successful that they are considered unique in the history of printmaking!

The Letter, one of the works in this series, was made with three separate plates. Mary inked the plates herself each time before they went through the printing press. She wanted to control the color carefully.

Although *The Letter* is not a woodblock print, the finished image clearly shows the Japanese influence. The model's desk is spare and angular, in keeping with the Japanese style. She sits close to the viewer but also close to the wall. There is no sense of depth in the room. This kind of flattened composition is common in Japanese art as are the boldly outlined forms and rich patterns.

In a later painting, *The Bath,* the Japanese influence is again seen. In this picture, however, something else is also powerful: the loving communication between the mother and her child. Although motherhood was a popular subject for artists in the late nineteenth century, Mary was able to paint this kind of relationship so tenderly that she became known for it throughout the world.

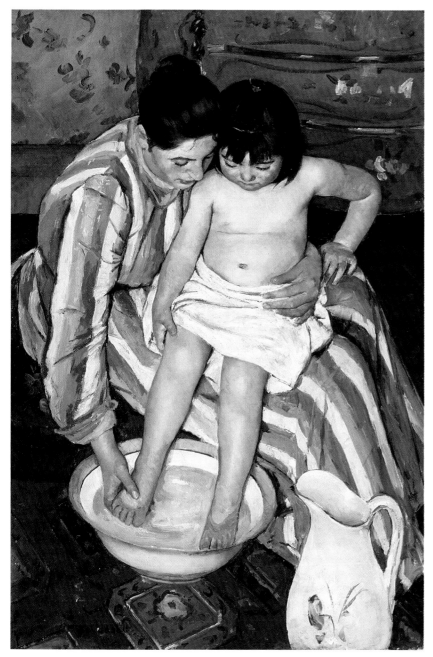

The Bath, 1891–92.

Maternal Caress (p. 11) also exhibits this talent of Mary's. The way in which the child looks into her mother's eyes and touches her face and the way the mother tightly holds her baby realistically capture this strong bond.

Painting mothers and their children, now a main theme for Mary, was her way to express her feelings about family life. Although she never married or had children, her family was extremely important to her. Perhaps that is why it was easy for her to understand the mother-child bond.

In the 1890s, Mary had many one-person exhibitions both in Europe and America. Though both her parents died during this decade, she continued to work, using her art to overcome her grief. She wrote to a friend, "I work, & that is the whole secret of anything like content with life, when everything else is gone." Her work sold so well now that, with the help of her inheritance, she was able to buy a large summer home outside of Paris. There she played with her small Belgian griffon dogs and entertained family and friends. Some of the most famous and important people of her day came to her parties. She also had over one thousand rose bushes, which she tended herself. She exclaimed after they were planted, "There is nothing like making pictures with real things!"

The Boating Party, 1893–94.

In 1893 and 1894, Mary painted one of her strongest works, *The Boating Party*. Captured in bright daylight, a young mother and child are being rowed by an oarsman dressed in dark blue. The colors are vivid. The forms are solid. As Degas often did, Mary added an element of mystery: most of the oarsman's face is hidden. She cut off the front part of the boat, a device which makes the viewer feel like a passenger. This bold composition suggests that Mary was more confident than ever.

Even though Mary had accomplished so much with her art, she was still dissatisfied with the lack of good paintings in America. She worked to change that. She helped her family and wealthy American friends collect art that they would eventually give to American museums. Now no American would have to feel as frustrated as Mary had.

Toward the end of Mary's life, she suffered from diabetes and was almost blind, but her fighting spirit remained strong. Although she stayed in France, she sent paintings to America to help support the campaign for women's voting rights. She also entertained young art students, delighting them with her "peppery" personality and strong opinions. She received many honors, too, like the Legion of Honor, a French award not usually given to women. Her old school, the Pennsylvania Academy of the Fine Arts, honored her as well. She usually refused awards, however, and *always* refused to be a juror of an art exhibition. She could remember too well how bad it felt to have her work judged and rejected.

Mary Cassatt took great risks. She chose to be a professional artist in an era when few women ever considered it. She joined the most radical artists of her time, the Impressionists, in their revolt against what they considered old-fashioned art. She then continued to develop her own independent art interests, particularly the private lives of women and mothers with children. She was an explorer and experimenter in printmaking and pastels as well as in painting. She pushed herself constantly, never letting herself be comfortable, never completely satisfying her own high standards. It is typical of her that six years before her death, she wrote to a close friend, "I have not done what I wanted to but I tried to make a good fight." Mary Stevenson Cassatt died at her summer home on June 14, 1926. Her fighting spirit helped to create art the world will long remember.

Leonora Carrington

Leonora Carrington, about age four.

Leonora Carrington was born in April 1917 to a wealthy family in Lancashire, in northern England. She was a strikingly beautiful child with dark hair and piercing dark eyes.

Leonora's mother, Maureen, was Irish. Her father, Harold, was a British businessman who owned factories that made cloth. She had three brothers, Pat, Gerard, and Arthur. While the boys were allowed to roughhouse, Leonora was expected to be proper and ladylike. Later she said that she resented being treated differently from her brothers.

Leonora was always interested in the unknown. At age four, when she became sick with a high fever, she felt that she left her bedroom and traveled to some mysterious other place. After she recovered, she was scared but also curious.

Leonora's mother and nanny fed her imagination by telling her fairy tales and Celtic (old Irish) legends about goddesses and about people and animals from other worlds. She learned about miracles and saints from nuns and a Roman Catholic priest. Their religious stories made Leonora want to perform supernatural feats like floating through the air. She felt so inspired that she wrote her own tales and illustrated them. Horses were one of her favorite subjects.

Although Leonora was intelligent and was also accomplished in piano, art, and horseback riding, she was asked to leave the first two schools she attended. Her teachers thought her impossible. She was always challenging and frustrating them with questions such as "Who said that two and two are four?" Furthermore, Leonora chose to write in such a way that her words could not be read. No one realized that her handwriting had to be held up to a mirror to be understood.

At fifteen, Leonora was sent to a boarding school in Florence, Italy. There she learned how to paint and studied some of the greatest art of the past. In the Uffizi Gallery of Florence and in Venice, Siena, and Rome, she was especially impressed by the fourteenth- and fifteenth-century paintings. This art often showed fantastic worlds where it seemed anything could happen. Leonora, who already believed in the existence of such places, now decided to become an artist.

Leonora's upper-class parents, however, wanted her to marry. In fact, her mother wanted her to marry

into the royal family of England! When Leonora was seventeen, she reluctantly agreed to become a debutante. At a large party, she was introduced to society as a woman ready for marriage. She attended many balls in London, sat near the royal family at the Ascot horse races, and was even formally presented to the king of England in a special ceremony. She despised these events, though. At the horse races she was so bored that she read a book.

As an adult, Leonora painted *Crookhey Hall* to express how she felt about her early life. Crookhey Hall was the name of her childhood home, a huge house where her parents employed ten servants and a chauffeur. In this painting, a woman, perhaps Leonora, frantically runs down a path as though she is trying to escape. Her skin, hair, and dress are ghost white. A dark, menacing figure floats behind her. Although some of the details of the picture may seem puzzling, it is clear that Leonora wanted to escape her family's way of life.

When Leonora told her parents of her artistic plans, they suggested she raise fox terriers instead! After much arguing, however, she was allowed to attend the Chelsea School of Art in London, England, and then a smaller school run by a man named Amédée Ozenfant. Ozenfant was very demanding. To teach Leonora how to draw, he had

Crookhey Hall, 1947.

her copy the same apple for a whole year using only a hard lead pencil.

One day a fellow student introduced Leonora to another painter, Max Ernst. Leonora knew about Ernst's work because her mother had given her an art book on the surrealists, a group to which he belonged. The surrealists were artists and writers who had formed a new art movement, surrealism, in France during the 1920s. Dedicated to the idea of freedom, they made up their own rules about how to live and what their art should be. They did not want their art to be realistic or to make sense in a logical way. They felt art should not be planned or thought out too much. Artists should be like children, totally free to play and make believe. In this way, the surrealists sought to explore and express the hidden thoughts of the mind. Sometimes they used their dreams and games of chance to make their art. The results were often mysterious images such as a melting clock, a cup and saucer made of fur, a woman with tree roots for veins.

Leonora was so taken with Ernst and the other surrealists that she quit art school and moved to Paris to join them. She was eager to be on her own and do what she wanted. Leonora's rebellious spirit led her in a different direction from her parents' wishes. To them, her behavior was shocking.

Ernst separated from his wife to be with Leonora. Soon, they moved to the south of France, where they lived for two years. It was an exciting and fruitful time. Leonora and Ernst supported and encouraged each other's work. Besides painting, they created cement sculptures of animals and mythological creatures, which they hung on their walls. Leonora wrote humorous stories that mocked her upbringing. She kept a garden and learned to cook.

The Inn of the Dawn Horse, or *Self-Portrait,* was painted during this period. It shows Leonora sitting in a chair that has arms and feet that resemble her own. A large white rocking horse, like one that she played with as a child, is suspended behind her as a realistic horse gallops away outdoors. To the side of Leonora is a hyena.

Leonora is looking forcefully at the viewer, but what is she saying? Perhaps her writings give some answers. In her play *Penelope,* a young girl is forbidden by her father from playing with her rocking horse. Rebelling, she turns into a beautiful white horse and escapes to a secret and magical world. Leonora had learned about magical white horses from the Celtic legends her mother and nanny had told her. In her story "The Debutante," a hyena dressed in a gown, high heels, and gloves takes the place of a young woman who does not want to attend a ball arranged by her parents. They discover the joke, however, when they detect a foul smell coming from the hyena. *The Inn of the Dawn Horse* is a surrealist fantasy. It reflects Leonora's sense of humor, rebellion, and desire for freedom.

Unfortunately, Leonora's "paradise time," as she once called it, ended in a horrible way. In September 1939, Germany invaded Poland. Two days later, France and England declared war on Germany, and World War II began. Ernst, who was German, was arrested in France and imprisoned in a concentration camp. For a time he was set free, but a few months later, he was arrested again. In despair, Leonora fled to Spain, which had not joined the war. There she

The Inn of the Dawn Horse [Self-Portrait], 1936–37.

collapsed and had to be hospitalized for a nervous breakdown.

Luckily, Leonora recovered. After several months, a nurse who was employed by her family took Leonora to Portugal, another neutral country. Her parents did not believe that she was completely well. They planned to send her to a hospital in South Africa, far from the European war zone.

Leonora didn't want to go. She slipped away from her nurse and called a friend, Renato Leduc, a Mexican diplomat temporarily assigned to Portugal. Leduc offered to marry Leonora. Because he was a diplomat, they could easily leave Europe. Leonora did see Ernst again. He had been released but was now involved with another woman. In 1941, Leonora and Leduc married and settled in New York City.

Leonora's drawing *Tiburón* shows her feelings about her journeys. A large shark, like a bizarre ship, carries passengers in its belly. Above its body are a girl sleeping in a bed that is on top of a wolf; a naked woman hanging upside-down under a floating chair; and two horses galloping through clouds that come from the shark's nose. Below the shark appear more strange images. Like a terrifying dream, *Tiburón* shows how fleeing the war and being in a psychiatric hospital must have felt.

After living in New York for about a year, Leonora and Leduc moved to Mexico City. Several of Leonora's surrealist friends from Europe settled in Mexico as well. One especially important woman friend was an artist named Remedios Varo. Leonora and Remedios saw each other practically every day. They both read widely about religion, mythology, philosophy, science, magic, and other subjects. They shared ideas, worked together on stories and plays,

Tiburón, about 1942.

and concocted fanciful recipes. They especially enjoyed magic and mischief. Once, for a party, they colored tapioca with black squid ink and served it as caviar!

In 1943, Leonora and Leduc divorced, but they remained friends. That same year, she met Emerico Weisz, nicknamed Chiki, a Hungarian photographer who had also fled Europe. They fell in love, married, and had two sons, Gabriel in 1946 and Pablo in 1947. Leonora loved having children and felt that being a mother helped her to be more creative.

Leonora painted *Baby Giant* while pregnant with Pablo. It shows a huge woman standing in a forest populated by tiny animals and hunters. Above the forest and going up to the sky is a blue-green sea filled with men in sailing vessels and various sea creatures. The woman wears a white cape that is open to reveal a red dress painted with imaginary figures, who, like ancient Egyptian gods and goddesses, have heads of animals and birds. Geese fly out from her cape. In her delicate hands, the woman carefully holds a speckled egg as if it were a precious jewel. Her young, innocent face is surrounded by glowing stalks of ripened wheat. She looks nothing like a scary giant!

While *Baby Giant* may show how big Leonora felt being pregnant, it also reflects her love of fairy tales, myths, and legends. Leonora had learned from Celtic legends and old religions that women used to be worshipped as goddesses. They were the source of great creative power. The egg was a sign or symbol of birth and creativity. In Egyptian myths, the goose was a goddess that gave birth to the sun. *Baby Giant,* like much of Leonora's art, is a message to women to reclaim their creative power and protect and nurture the universe.

Baby Giant shows, too, how Leonora's painting technique changed in Mexico. Before, she had been

Baby Giant, about 1947.

working with oil paints. Now she experimented with water-based tempera paint as well, grinding the colors and mixing in egg yolk. Using this traditional egg tempera method on wood panels with a smooth, white coating made her paintings look deep and glowing, as if lit from within.

Since her early years in Mexico, Leonora has also experimented with other media. She likes to paint freely, using the images that spontaneously come to her. Because she is ambidextrous, she sometimes paints with both hands at once! Still, careful drawing is the basis for all her work. She pays great attention to details and often uses tiny brushes.

Leonora's art had been shown in surrealist exhibits since 1938. It was not until after her one-woman show in New York City in 1948, however, that Mexican galleries began to pay attention. In 1963, the Mexican government asked her to paint a mural for the new museum of anthropology in Mexico City. She painted *The Magic World of the Maya* about the Chiapas Indians, descendants of the ancient Mayan people. To prepare, Leonora visited the Chiapas in southern Mexico, riding a horse or a mule part way. Forbidden by the Indians to use a camera, she recorded their lives by drawing. Her mural shows their habits and beliefs interpreted through her own imagination.

Leonora Carrington in her Mexico City studio, about 1944.

Step-Sister's Hen (or *Marigold, Marigold,
Tell Me Your Answer Do),* 1952.

As Leonora paints and writes, she continues to interweave her knowledge of religions and myths with her childhood fascinations. She loves songs and sometimes uses them to title her work. In *Step-Sister's Hen,* also named *Marigold, Marigold, Tell Me Your Answer Do,* she refers to an old song, "A Bicycle Built for Two." Its chorus begins, "Daisy, Daisy, give me your answer, do." Leonora substituted the marigold because some Mexicans place marigolds on the graves of dead people with whom they want to communicate. They believe that when people die, they lose their ability to see all colors except the yellow of marigolds. Using marigolds is a way to bring back a dead person's spirit.

In Leonora's painting, a marigoldlike creature with a starstruck expression stands in a blue chamber. She holds a thin black cord attached to the collar of a bright reddish-orange hen with long black hair. The hen is shedding feathers and appears angry. Above these two creatures floats an upside-down white form whose shape echoes that of the marigold. A similar form is on the wall. Outside, in the distance, is a brownish-red landscape with deer or horses, or perhaps a unicorn.

This painting, like most of Leonora's art, is a riddle. It asks questions it does not answer. Does it reflect Leonora's childhood desire to float through

Grandmother Moorhead's Aromatic Kitchen, 1975.

the air? Are the white forms spirits of the dead? Is it about communication between the dead and the living? "Images arise," Leonora says. "I don't know from where. They just arise."

Grandmother Moorhead's Aromatic Kitchen is another mysterious painting. Grandmother Moorhead was Leonora's maternal grandmother. In this kitchen, a huge white goose, like that of Mother Goose, is in charge. She may also be a goddess from a Celtic legend. Her helper is a horned creature that resembles some animal gods in ancient myths. Five ghostlike figures are cooking a traditional Mexican meal. On the floor is a circle of black lines. If held up to a mirror, they reveal Celtic writing about an underworld where a goddess reigns. Painting a kitchen scene is particularly fitting for Leonora. She

Red Cow, 1989.

thought of painting and cooking as ways to transform everyday materials into something extraordinary. She once said, "Painting is like making strawberry jam—really carefully and well."

In the 1970s, Leonora helped start the women's rights movement in Mexico. She also spoke publicly about her belief that plants and animals are as important as people and that women must keep harmony among all life forms. Gradually, Leonora's art, shown in many international exhibits, became known throughout the world. She once said, however, "I painted for myself. I never believed that anyone would exhibit or buy my work."

Red Cow is a painting which combines Leonora's many concerns. In some ancient cultures, the cow was considered to be a goddess whose milk formed the milky way. Her colors were red, white, and black.

Here, a large fire-red cow with a white face and hooves and black eyes earnestly stares into space. She is in a bleak but magical setting. A grey building similar to Crookhey Hall stands in the background. In front are some black ravens. To the left of the cow, but slightly behind it, stand two shadowy figures. One looks like a priest, and the other may be a small child. The night sky is dark blue and studded with stars.

The cow looks out wistfully, as if in want of change. Perhaps she, like Leonora, is searching for a spiritual world.

Leonora Carrington sees the invisible. Rebelling against her family's expectations, she is like the character in her book *The Hearing Trumpet,* who says, "I have always refused to give up that wonderful strange power I have inside me." Using fairy tales, legends, myths, and religious teachings as her sources, she creates surrealist fantasies with otherworldly creatures. The power of women is particularly important as it is the force which creates and nurtures life. Leonora uses her art for exploration. "Painting is my vehicle of transit," she has said. "I don't always know where I am going or what it means."

Betye Saar

Betye Saar in 1928, at age two.

As a young child, Betye Saar liked to search for treasure in her grandmother's backyard. She dug in the dirt with a stick, uncovering bits of glass, stones, and beads, special objects to add to her collection of treasures. These treasure hunts foretold Betye's future. Looking for and collecting objects would become the way that she made art.

Betye (whose name is pronounced the same as "Betty") was born in 1926 to Beatrice and Jefferson Brown. She grew up in Pasadena, California. Her summers were spent with her grandmother in Watts, then a rural area of Los Angeles. There an Italian immigrant named Simon Rodia was creating a remarkable work of art, the Watts Towers, out of things he found. He built eight tall, cone-shaped spirals from steel rods which he covered with concrete. He then placed in the concrete thousands of rocks, shells, bottle caps, and small pieces of glass, broken pottery, mirrors, and tile. To Betye, who passed the towers on her way to and from the grocery store, they were "a fairy-tale palace."

Betye liked to create, too, and often did art projects with her mother, brother, and sister. Her mother, Beatrice, who made clothes for a living, gave her children clay, crayons, paper, and paste with which to work. Sometimes they all took crafts classes together at their local park.

Betye's father, Jefferson, was an especially strong influence. He was a salesman who liked to sketch and to write plays and songs. He believed there is a spirit or energy that connects all living things.

According to Beatrice, Betye had spiritual powers: she could "see things" that others could not. Once she surprised her mother by saying, "Daddy's angry because he missed the streetcar." When Jefferson arrived home late from work, he *was* annoyed. Betye was right! He had just missed the streetcar.

When Betye was six years old, her life changed dramatically. Her father died from a kidney ailment. Betye could not understand why he had left. She felt "as if a door had shut." She lost her special power to see things. Although she did not realize it, she was full of anger; she felt that her father had abandoned her. Later, when she made art, images of death often appeared in her work.

Eventually Beatrice married again and had two more children, a girl and a boy. This was during the Great Depression, a time in America when many

Rainbow Babe in the Woods (1979) shows Betye as a child.

33

Baby, 1932.

lacked enough money to live. Luckily, Beatrice and her new husband, Emmett, both had jobs.

While their parents were working, the children amused themselves by doing crafts projects such as making puppets or doll furniture. If they could not think of what to do, they would look in a book on crafts for children. Sometimes they recycled their dolls and other toys by painting them to look new. Betye especially loved making gifts. Creating, for her, was a way to give people pleasure.

In the 1940s, Betye attended Pasadena City College, where she was an excellent student. As an African-American, though, she was never asked to join the art club or the honorary society for talented art students. Once her design for a parade float won an award, but she was not given the prize she deserved. This discrimination angered Betye. Years later, she said her anger pushed her to work harder.

In 1949, Betye graduated from the University of California at Los Angeles and became a social worker. When she was twenty-six, she married another artist, Richard Saar. They had three daughters. In the 1950s and early 1960s, she worked as a designer and a jewelry maker while bringing up her children. Sometimes they created along with her.

In 1956, Betye discovered a love of printmaking. She had returned to school to earn a teaching certificate in design. In a print class, she began making color etchings of children and nature. Although Betye enjoyed this process and won some awards, she did not yet think of herself as an artist. Having been discriminated against as an African-American, she found it difficult to believe she *could* be an artist. Her printmaking teacher, however, encouraged her.

Although Betye and her husband divorced in 1968, she had a positive experience that year which profoundly affected her work. She saw an exhibition by an artist named Joseph Cornell. Cornell used boxes with glass fronts to create miniature theaters. He would place objects he had collected in the boxes to make unusual, small worlds. Seeing Cornell's technique gave Betye, also a collector, a direction for developing her art.

Betye had already been framing her prints and drawings within windows. *Black Girl's Window* represents her autobiography, "myself as a shadow

Black Girl's Window, 1969.

looking through a window." This shadow girl is flat and undefined. Only her eyes are clearly visible, one open, one closed, as if she is both looking out at the world and looking inside herself. Pressed up against the windowpane, she seems to yearn for escape.

Betye may have used a window because she believes that art is a kind of window. Through it, an artist can reveal inner thoughts and feelings. The viewer can, in turn, see inside the artist.

Many of the images in this work relate to magic and fortune-telling: the girl's hands, the stars, moons, and suns. The skeleton and the wolf baying at the moon are Tarot cards, used by fortune tellers to predict the future. In the center is the skeleton, or death. "Everything revolves around death," Betye has said. Together, these images show the girl's fate.

At the bottom of the three rows of pictures is an old photograph of a white woman from the middle 1800s. Betye had white ancestors in both her parents' families. She says that she understands the double feeling of being both black and white.

Soon Betye began to make box sculptures, too. Deeply angered by the murder of the civil rights leader Dr. Martin Luther King, Jr., in 1968, Betye used boxes to make strong political statements. For years, she had been collecting negative images of

The Liberation of Aunt Jemima, 1972.

African-Americans such as Aunt Jemima. Aunt Jemima was a fat, smiling, African-American character invented by advertisers to sell pancake mix. She looked like a white person's idea of what a kitchen slave should be: cheerful, generous, helpful, an expert in the kitchen who knew her place. Betye felt that this stereotypical image was offensive and deeply upsetting.

She created *The Liberation of Aunt Jemima,* one of her most famous works, to confront this insult. Betye took pancake box labels showing Aunt Jemima's face and pasted them like wallpaper on the inside back of a box. In front, she placed an Aunt Jemima doll holding a miniature broom and toy pistol in one hand and a toy rifle and toy hand grenade in the other. In front of the doll, there is a postcard showing an Aunt Jemima carrying a crying white infant. A clenched black fist, the emblem of the Black Power movement, covers her skirt. The work is a strong warning: violence can erupt when people are not treated as human beings.

In 1974, Betye began to do art about her family history. Her work became softer and more delicate. She created *Record for Hattie* to express her love of her great-aunt Hattie and to celebrate the life of a real African-American woman, not a false one like Aunt Jemima. Aunt Hattie, who died in 1974 at

Record for Hattie, 1975.

the age of ninety-eight, had been like a dear, loving grandmother to her. In a beautiful old wooden box, Betye placed many of the things that Hattie had used and collected: a pearl necklace, a hand mirror, a pincushion, an egg timer, an autograph book from Hattie's childhood, a dried rose, rosettes from stockings, and a small cross. All of these objects reflect Hattie's personality and life, her skill, care, devotion, and beauty.

Although Betye believes anything can be used to make art, she prefers certain kinds of materials. She likes old things that have "a feeling of being used and having gone through someone's lifetime" because they "have secrets of where they've been before, people that they're related to." She believes that each object "has a certain energy from its previous function that carries over into its new use." By putting objects together, Betye combines the different energies to produce a new object with greater energy. Betye calls this process "power-gathering."

The idea of powerful objects is common in places where people live in tribes. In such tribal cultures, artworks are used as fetishes, or magical tools, to help people live through important events such as births, deaths, or illnesses.

While Betye is attracted to the art of many tribal cultures, she is particularly drawn to traditional African sculpture. This art combines two kinds of objects. One, like fabric or beads, is used for decoration. The other, like the teeth, fur, bone, or hooves of an animal, is added for power. Betye decided that in her work she would choose which materials were for decoration and which for power.

The shapes of Betye's pieces also communicate power. Even before making sculptures about her family, Betye had begun to mount her boxes on tables. Sometimes they formed a pyramid shape, used in ancient civilizations to express power. Often they resembled religious altars where people come to make an offering to a god.

Indigo Mercy is an example of one of her altarpieces. It is also an *assemblage,* or sculpture of many parts. The top is an old clock case which sits on a table made from palm-tree leaves. Inside the case is a mysterious figure, a rag doll that has been transformed by many added objects. For its face, Betye used a painted mask that is either Mexican or Native-American. Its eyes are *milagros,* or "miracles," charms that are hung in Mexican churches to ask for a special blessing or miracle. Betye added extra hair and bits of broken mirror in the background. For the arms she attached iguana paws from key chains, possibly also from Mexico. The dress is African fabric and lizard skin. It is decorated with wooden buttons, a key, feathers, yarn, charms, and a fragment from a Persian rug.

This transformed doll is like a fetish. It has decorative elements—yarn, paint, and fabric—as well as power elements—hair, claws, and lizard skin. It is somewhat frightening but also engaging. It has a mysterious energy, as if it were alive.

Indigo Mercy (detail), 1975.

Betye finds her objects in thrift shops, flea markets, and other places throughout the world. She is always searching, as she did as a child, for interesting "refuse." While she saves things for the right time to use them, it is not unusual for her to wait for the right piece to appear. She says that, for her, creating is a "slow, patient process."

Once she had almost finished a sculpture except for a blank space in the center. She did not know what was needed but knew something special was required. Instead of using an object that she wasn't satisfied with, she decided to be patient and have faith. About a year later, she went hiking in the mountains with some friends. While they walked on one side of the mountain, something told Betye to choose a different path. She was hiking alone when she lost her balance and slid briefly. There, in front of her, was a "bleached white bone," "like a little special throne," the perfect piece for her sculpture's center. She knew the bone did not appear by accident because there were very few animals in that area.

Betye had trusted her strong feelings, her intuition. "It's like an inner voice that tells me what to do. And the more I rely on that voice, the stronger it becomes." Chance also helps. "The element of risk, the element of the unknown . . . that's where the spirit comes in."

The Watts Towers.

Spirit Catcher is another work that brings together various objects from different cultures, combining their separate energies to make a new and stronger statement. Betye collected objects for this piece for three years. Its spiral shape and lacy structure are similar to the Watts Towers, but it is made of bamboo, rattan, sticks, and string. The base is a rattan table. Surrounding a cross-shaped bamboo form are little ladders. Various articles are attached to this basic structure: the painted skull of a bird, pierced by a hatpin; bones painted with decorative leopard spots; shells; feathers; the emblems of several religions. At the very top is a Moroccan purse with a mirror. The mirror is like an eye, both all-seeing and protective, scaring away bad spirits. Betye also included small bags of incense for smell and movable rattles and chimes for sound.

Spirit Catcher is modeled after a spirit trap from Tibet, a region of China. In Tibet, these bamboo traps are placed on the tops of houses to catch spirits, good ones and bad ones. They are supposed to save the good spirits for good luck and hold the bad spirits to keep them from hurting anyone. Betye's *Spirit Catcher* is like Betye. She, too, captures and uses spiritual energy.

Betye's sculpture *Mti* (pronounced "mm tee") communicates spirit in another way. (*Mti,* or

"wood," is a word from Swahili, an African language.) Like *Indigo Mercy* and *Spirit Catcher, Mti* is an altarpiece constructed of objects from different cultures and religions. This piece, however, is unlike Betye's other work because she invited viewers to contribute their own objects to it. *Mti,* like some religious altars, constantly changes as new people come and add their gifts: poems, toys, coins, candles, charms—whatever they want. Betye feels that with each person's offering, his or her spirit is contributed, too, allowing the spiritual energy of many people to mix and grow stronger.

The experience of *Mti* encouraged Betye to create larger art pieces—*installations*—which are like decorated rooms, or environments, that people can enter and participate in. Betye constructed *House of Gris Gris* with her daughter Alison Saar, also an artist. A gris-gris is an African charm believed to have magic powers. The house is a small cottage with wire-mesh walls stuffed with moss, twigs, and pleasant-smelling eucalyptus leaves. Light shines like stars through the roof's tiny holes. Old bottles of different sizes and shapes decorate the interior. Outside the house float metal wings attached to a harness. A pile of metal objects, resembling human hearts, sits nearby on the floor. From another room comes a rasping sound.

Spirit Catcher, 1976–77.

Betye with *Mti,* 1988.

House of Gris Gris seems haunted! There are no visible ghosts, but the smells, sounds, and materials all create the feeling that someone once lived there.

For a lot of people, Betye's work is strange. Like most original artists and particularly African-American women artists, she had to struggle for acceptance. At times she joined with others for support and encouragement. Gradually Betye

House of Gris Gris (1990) by Betye Saar and Alison Saar.

Guardian of Desires, 1988.

received more and more recognition, not just within the African-American and women's art communities but within the larger art world, too.

In 1975, Betye was asked to have a solo exhibition at the prestigious Whitney Museum of American Art in New York City. She had also begun to win awards. These were great honors, but to Betye, *real* success is "doing a piece that I like" and "to . . . love what I'm doing."

In 1987, Betye became an artist-in-residence for one year at the Massachusetts Institute of Technology. There, for the first time, she was exposed to scientific objects like the circuit boards used in computers. While these materials were seemingly unrelated to her earlier work, Betye found a way to include them.

Guardian of Desires shows her use of these new technological objects along with her old "found" ones. A mysterious cat stands in front of a wall that is really a black and silver circuit board. The black cat's body is a crushed paintbrush that Betye found in the street on the way to her studio, combined with a carved cat's head from Mexico. Inside the cat's mouth is a skull. When she put the figure in front of the circuit board, she added a cigar holder and filled it with circuit-board wire and beads. The reverse side of the piece has milagros arranged in the shape of a figure: eyes, heart, arms, hands, and legs.

How different these objects become when combined! The circuit board, with its metallic circles and wires, now looks like a night sky filled with stars and constellations. Betye thinks of the circuit board as "information about the unknown." The entire piece, standing on a found, paint-splattered wooden base, feels like it comes from another world, a world that science cannot explain.

Betye Saar gives recycling a larger meaning, transforming ordinary, often discarded materials into extraordinary works of art. Reflecting the lives and spirit of many people, these materials possess an energy. Betye captures and combines their energy to create artwork charged with spiritual power. The viewer feels connected to her work whether she is using objects from Africa, Asia, Mexico, the Caribbean, or the United States. In Betye Saar's art, all peoples, all races, are united.

Mary Frank

Mary Frank, about age fourteen.

When Mary Frank was a young girl in an English boarding school, she was asked to do something she felt was unthinkable. Her teacher gave all the students boxes with poison and told them to catch and kill butterflies. World War II had begun. Butterflies were eating cabbages needed for soldiers. Mary didn't want to harm a butterfly. Instead, she decided she would just stop eating cabbage. This solution tells a lot about her. Originality, determination, and respect for life are all qualities she would exhibit as an artist.

Born in London, England, on February 4, 1933, Mary was the only child of Eleanore and Edward Lockspeiser. Her mother was a painter who, Mary said, painted "as if her life depended on it." Her father wrote about music, poetry, and art.

As a child, Mary learned to keep her feelings to herself. Her many stuffed animals became her companions. She also enjoyed reading, particularly sad fairy tales like Hans Christian Andersen's "The Snow Queen" and "The Marsh King's Daughter."

She remembers crying so much that her fairy-tale book got wet and had to be dried out on the radiator.

Sometimes Mary's mother would take time to be with her. She made puppets and clothes for Mary's dolls. She would also play the piano while Mary danced freely, twirling silk scarves. Dancing gave Mary wonderful feelings of pleasure. She was sensitive to her body and loved how she felt when she was moving.

Like Betye Saar, Mary experienced drastic changes when she was six years old. England declared war on Germany in 1939, and London was in danger of being bombed. To be safe, most children living in the cities were sent to boarding schools in the countryside. Mary's parents sent her, too. It was a frightening time, partly because Mary didn't understand why she was being sent away.

Because of the almost constant threat of bombs, Mary had to move from one school to another. All the schools she attended were Christian, but Mary was Jewish. She felt like an outsider.

Even more upsetting, she hardly ever saw her parents. They did not visit often because they, too, needed to move many times to remain safe. Their house, in fact, was bombed and all of Mary's mother's paintings were destroyed.

By 1940, when Mary was seven, Eleanore decided that the two of them must go to the United States, where Mary's grandparents lived. Mary's father stayed in England to help put out fires caused by bombings in the war. For a while, she missed him terribly. She wrote him many letters and often enclosed her drawings. Gradually, however, Mary became involved in her new life and stopped thinking so much about him. In four years, Eleanore and Edward would divorce. Mary would see her father only four more times.

In America, Mary lived with her mother, two aunts, and grandparents in a big house in Brooklyn, New York. Again, she went to different schools. Her mother and grandfather could not agree which one was best. With her British accent, Mary felt odd. Soon, however, she learned to speak like her classmates.

Dance now became Mary's main interest. She wanted to study it, but her school, the High School for Music and Art, didn't have a dance program. Mary studied art instead and took dance classes outside of school.

Eleanore was excited about Mary's art studies. While she never pushed her daughter in her academic subjects, she gave her chisels for sculpting wood and encouraged whatever artistic effort she made. Mary admired her mother's dedication to art and learned from her how satisfying making art can be. Yet, she wasn't sure she liked having a mother who was an artist. Often Eleanore was too busy painting to spend time with Mary.

The one time Eleanore gave Mary an art lesson, it was a disaster. To teach Mary a basic rule of composition, she asked her to draw three separate things. When Mary put one of them, a tree, in the center of the paper, Eleanore explained that this wasn't right. The composition should not be symmetrical. Mary was furious! She refused to change her picture. She wanted to do things her way, not to follow someone else's rules.

Mary did enjoy their trips to the Metropolitan Museum of Art. Most of all, she loved the Egyptian art. She particularly remembers a wooden sculpture of a boy with one leg in front of the other as if he were walking. He was less than ten inches tall, yet carved with such ''tenderness and delicacy,'' Mary says, that he has haunted her to this day.

Mary also spent many hours looking at her mother's art books and magazines. In a magazine called *Verve,* there was a photograph of a clay doll's head from India. It was a small head, no more than two inches high. Its eyes were just slits. Nevertheless, Mary deeply understood the doll's sad expression.

By 1949, dancing was so important to Mary that she convinced her mother to let her change schools and enter the Professional Children's School, where she could major in dance. She studied with the legendary dancer and choreographer Martha Graham. Graham was a passionate woman who believed that the shapes dancers form can express powerful emotions. Working with her, Mary learned to appreciate movement and gesture as ways to communicate her feelings.

Although Mary loved her studies, she soon realized that she would never be a professional dancer or choreographer. She knew how much these artists sacrificed and was too curious about life to devote so many hours to practicing. She had also met a man, Robert Frank, with whom she wanted to spend a lot of time. Frank was a dedicated photographer whose pictures were quickly gaining much public attention. He and Mary fell in love. In 1950, when she was seventeen, they married. At eighteen, she had their son, Pablo, and three years later, a daughter, Andrea.

After giving up her ambitions as a dancer, Mary returned to art. For a while, she carved wood in the studio of a friend. Sometimes she worked on her fire escape. She also tried to see as many art exhibits as possible. Once she was married and had children, it was more difficult to find time. She and the children traveled with Robert while he photographed Europe and the American West. Yet Mary continued to work whenever she could. In Paris, she visited the Louvre Museum, where she made drawings inspired by the art. She was particularly attracted to ancient art: Etruscan, Greek, Middle Eastern, and Oriental.

When the Franks were back in New York City, Mary took drawing classes. Wherever she went, she carried a sketchbook and drew the people or animals around her. In the summers, the Franks lived on Cape Cod, Massachusetts, where Mary would draw at the beach. She liked to put her head on the sand, "eye down on the level of the snake," to see how people looked nearby and far away. A hand or a leg close to her seemed huge, while a person in the distance appeared tiny. People lost their personal identities and became timeless figures moving through endless space.

Andrea and Pablo, 1962.

Sometimes Mary would have friends help her carry logs from the beach for carving. She liked to carve because "in wood, you have time to make thousands of choices with each cut. You're like an animal gnawing away at something." Her wooden sculptures were simple shapes that looked like people or animals. Mary also used arrows, rainbows, and an Eskimo statue as sources. Sometimes she got ideas at the American Museum of Natural History.

She experimented with different materials, too, such as plaster, wax, cement, and bronze. Often her pieces were imaginary people, half-woman and half-animal, creatures from mythology, and figures in motion.

In the 1950s, however, the art world was not very interested in work using the human figure. Mary was totally involved in her art and did not let the opinions of others influence her. Then, in 1958, she was asked to be in a two-person exhibition when one artist withdrew. Gradually, more and more people noticed and liked Mary's art. In the 1960s, she won awards and was written about in art magazines and newspapers. Soon she was asked to show in several galleries and has been represented by a well-known one ever since.

In 1969, Mary and Robert Frank began living apart and soon divorced. Mary moved to a large building for artists only and supported herself by teaching at a nearby college.

Also in 1969, Mary started to work with clay, which perfectly suited her way of creating. When Mary begins a piece, she may have a definite idea but no detailed plan. She likes to stay open to inspiration, chance, her materials, and the moment. She works quickly, to catch the movement, energy, and spirit of life. With wood or other hard materials, it is difficult to work so fast. Clay, however, responds to the touch. It is soft and bends easily, allowing Mary to be spontaneous with her material and ideas—to play.

In an early clay sculpture, *Journey,* a lifelike head, tilted upward, emerges from the base of a hill or mountainside. On top of the hill are two smaller figures, one crouching and headless, the other riding a horse. From the opposite side, the sculpture looks entirely different, more like a thin sheet of clay than a heavy mass. Cut out of the sheet is the profile of another head, one that recalls the clay doll's head Mary loved as a child. The open cut leads to a dark, cavelike space.

The experience of viewing *Journey* is similar to Mary's experience at the beach. People appear and disappear in space. Their scale changes. Mary decides how big to make her figures by what feels right to

Journey, 1970.

her and by how she imagines other people would feel. "I don't think that anyone feels his head to be necessarily the size it actually is," she says. "It depends on mood, on what one is doing, on the time of day."

Journey, like most of Mary's work, cannot be easily explained. Mary, in fact, wants her art to be open to different interpretations by different people or by the same person seeing the work at different times, from different angles, and in different light. She feels the work is richer then and more like life, which is always changing.

In 1973, Mary bought a house in the Catskill Mountains of New York State, where she lives in the warm months. Her home is surrounded by forests, woodland animals, and flower gardens. This nurturing environment is a setting for her art as well. Sitting among the trees, her sculptures may shelter a mouse or a bird.

Walking Woman could have been born there. Like the small wood carving of the Egyptian boy, she is frozen in motion, with one leg placed in front of the other. She bends forward, as if propelled by some pressing need. Her body appears tense and alert, her face, troubled.

Rough plaster covers most of her body. Her arms turn into sprays of branches and air, like wings. Stick

51

Running Man/
Walking Woman, 1981.

ribs jut out. Ferns, birchbark, and living vines cling to her. *Walking Woman* merges with nature. She reflects Mary's strong belief that trees, plants, air, light, people—*everything* is connected.

Although Mary continued to work mostly in clay, she wanted to make larger sculptures than are usually possible with this soft material. Large clay pieces tend to droop or fall. Mary's brilliant solution was to make her sculptures in small parts that could be placed next to one another, forming a whole image. To support these parts, she may use slabs of clay within the bodies of her figures, like skeletons holding muscles. Often the supports show, adding to the overall feeling of a piece.

Woman is one of her clay figures in parts. She is larger than life-size, lying on her back, knees bent, arms raised and crossed as if to protect herself. Her ribs seem to be coming out of her body, as though she is decaying. Fossils of ferns cover her chest. Her face wears an expression of grief and terror, one eye wide open, the other missing. Half of her face is featureless and blank. It is as if this woman, who is lying on the ground, is beginning to be taken back by the earth.

Mary in her New York City studio (1987 or 1988).

Woman, 1975.

In 1974, Mary's daughter, Andrea, died in a plane crash in a Central American jungle. She was only twenty years old. Mary was overcome with sorrow. Whatever she tried to create, like her sculpture *Woman,* reflected her memory of Andrea. In 1975, both her mother, Eleanore, and her son, Pablo, became seriously ill. The only way Mary could escape her grief was to draw "from life, from a model, a plant, from something that didn't feel so aware."

Horse and Rider is a sculpture made a few years later. It, too, expresses strong emotions. A small clay man, the rider, straddles two horses, which seem to be moving very fast. The wide-eyed man looks

Horse and Rider, 1982.

frantic. With one arm, he reaches forward to hold on. At the same time, he twists his head to look backward, as if he sees someone or something chasing him. The folded clay slabs create the effect of dust blown by the horses' galloping hooves.

Like horses and riders created for centuries, Mary's sculpture tells of an ancient theme: human beings are travelers through life. The passage is frightening. The horses with their skeletonlike eyeholes are a reminder of death.

Slowly, Mary's grief lessened. In 1984, she fell in love with Leo Treitler, a pianist and scholar of music. Their love as well as the passing of time helped Mary to recover from her tragedy. *Utterance* reflects this change. A tall, elegant woman, cloaked in a flowing clay gown, caringly watches a miniature horse walk away on her extended arm. Her downcast eyes and parted lips speak of sadness and love. She is letting go of the horse just as Mary was letting go of her pain.

Like so much of Mary's work, *Utterance* has a timeless feeling. Her choice of clay, often used in ancient art, contributes to this effect. The small horse resembles an antique Greek statue. The woman's head is similar to the Indian doll's head Mary admired as a child.

The entire piece feels delicate, like an angel. Yet it

Utterance, 1984.

Utterance (detail), 1984.

is made of a material from the earth—clay. *Utterance* is also rough. The gown's edges are torn. The slabs of clay were put together quickly. Mary left the supportive structure visible. She never disguises her materials or hides the traces of her process.

Since 1986, Mary has concentrated on drawing, painting, and printmaking. She has filled over a hundred sketchbooks with drawings of the world around her. She especially loves the challenge of trying to capture people and animals in motion. She compares doing this to "being a hunter." "It is very hard to catch them in motion like that, you have to work so fast. . . . but when you come near it, your work is injected with the life they have." Sometimes she even sketches actors performing in a darkened theater. This way, she is not always in control and so "not as likely to fall into the trap of habit."

Monoprints are important to Mary, too. They are made by painting on a flat, slick surface called a plate, then pressing a piece of paper on top of it. The paper picks up a reverse image. Making monoprints suits Mary's spontaneous style. She *must* work fast or the paint will dry. As with clay, the image can be easily changed. Colors can be added, layered, or wiped away. There are so many possibilities that surprises often occur. With monoprints, she says, "Anything can happen."

Self-portrait, 1990.

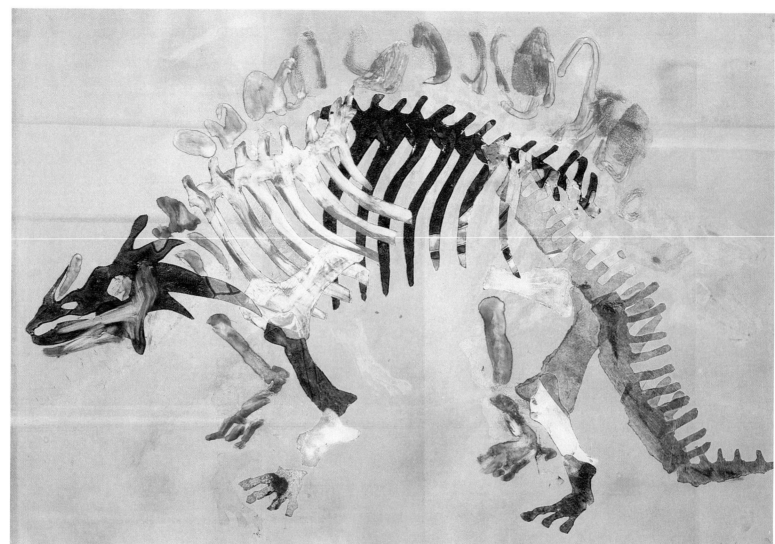

Dinosaur,
1980.

Dinosaur is one of a series of monoprints taken from sketches Mary did at the American Museum of Natural History. Mary has never made a sculpture of a dinosaur because, she feels, a dinosaur skeleton is already a great sculpture, "probably one of the best that's ever been." In this monoprint, she has caught the creature's enormous energy. The skeleton seems about to pounce. The movement is created by the patterns of color. There are even faded white bones, like ghosts. The ancient animal with its layers of paint also is a reminder of the passage of time.

Inspired by her blooming garden, Mary made monoprints of flowers. As her work developed, she felt a need to use more color. In this flower print, the bright colors against a dark background give the feeling of heavenly bodies as much as plants.

Always imaginative, original, and open to trying anything with her work, Mary Frank has created art as complex as life. She says it is about "what I feel it is to be human." She searches for images "strong enough to put all the feelings I have in. Sometimes I have the image of a ship that could be loaded up [with feelings] and could move through time."

Like the ancient art she loves, Mary's work is timeless. With her deep understanding of gesture, she makes her materials dance. Using clay and paint, paper and plaster, Mary creates people and animals that seem to move. Mary Frank takes the spirit of life and transforms it into art.

Flowers, 1991.

Picture Credits

Mary Cassatt

6   Copyprint of a photograph of an engraving (detail) (1854) by Peter Baumgaertner. Frederick Arnold Sweet Papers. Archives of American Art, Smithsonian Institution. Owner of original unknown.

8   Carte de visite (c. 1872). Photographers: Baroni and Gardelli. Albumen print. Courtesy of the Pennsylvania Academy of the Fine Arts, Philadelphia.

9   *A Mandolin Player* (c. 1868). Oil on canvas, 36¼″ × 29″. Philadelphia Museum of Art. Accession number: 10-1960-6. Private Collection.

11   *Maternal Caress* (c. 1896). Oil on canvas, 15″ × 21¼″. Philadelphia Museum of Art. Accession number: '70-75-2. Gift of Aaron E. Carpenter.

12   Edgar Degas, *Mary Cassatt at the Louvre* (1885). Handcolored etching; plate: 30.5 cm. × 12.6 cm. The Art Institute of Chicago. Gift of Kate L. Brewster Estate, 1949.515. Photograph © 1992, The Art Institute of Chicago. All Rights Reserved.

13   *At the Theatre* (c. 1879). Pastel on paper, 21¹³⁄₁₆″ × 18⅛″. The Nelson-Atkins Museum of Art, Kansas City, Missouri. (Anonymous Gift) F77-33.

14   *Lydia at a Tapestry Loom* (c. 1881). Oil on canvas, 25⅝″ × 36⅜″. Courtesy of the Flint Institute of Arts. Gift of The Whiting Foundation. (67.32).

15   *The Map*, or *The Lesson* (1889). Drypoint, second state, 6¼″ × 9³⁄₁₆″. The Metropolitan Museum of Art. Bequest of Mrs. H.O. Havemeyer, 1929. The H.O. Havemeyer Collection. (29.107.93). All rights reserved, The Metropolitan Museum of Art.

16   *The Letter* (c. 1891). Drypoint, soft-ground etching, and aquatint in color. Sheet: .446 m. × .275 m. (17⁹⁄₁₆″ × 10¹³⁄₁₆″). National Gallery of Art, Washington, D.C. Rosenwald Collection. (1950.1.40 (B-15919)).

17   *The Bath* (1891–92). Oil on canvas, 39½″ × 26″. The Art Institute of Chicago. Robert A. Waller Fund, 1910.2. Photograph © 1992, The Art Institute of Chicago. All Rights Reserved.

18   *The Boating Party* (1893-94). Oil on canvas, 0.902 m. × 1.171 m. (35½″ × 46⅛″). National Gallery of Art, Washington, D.C. Chester Dale Collection. (1963.10.94 (1758)).

Leonora Carrington

All art below: © 1993 Leonora Carrington/ARS, New York. All images courtesy of Dr. Salomón Grimberg.

20   Leonora Carrington at about age four. Photographer unknown. Private collection.

22   *Crookhey Hall* (1947). Casein on masonite, 31.5 cm. × 60 cm. Private collection.

24   *The Inn of the Dawn Horse* [*Self-Portrait*] (1936–37). Oil on canvas, 65 cm. × 81.2 cm. Private collection.

25   *Tiburón* (c. 1942). Indian ink and gouache, 9¾″ × 12⅝″ (25 cm. × 32 cm.). Private collection.

26   *Baby Giant* (c. 1947). Egg tempera on panel, 46¼″ × 26⅞″ (117.5 cm. × 68.5 cm.). Private collection.

27   Leonora Carrington in her studio, Mexico City (c. 1944). Photograph by Chiki Weisz. Private collection.

28   *Step-Sister's Hen* (or *Marigold, Marigold, Tell Me Your Answer Do*) (1952). Mixed oil and tempera on three-ply, 91.5 cm. × 52 cm. Private collection.

29   *Grandmother Moorhead's Aromatic Kitchen* (1975). Oil on canvas, 31″ × 49″. Charles B. Goddard Center for Visual and Performing Arts, Ardmore, Oklahoma.

2,30   *Red Cow* (1989). Oil on canvas, 24″ × 36″. Private collection.

Betye Saar

32   Betye Saar at age two (1928). Photograph. Courtesy of Betye Saar.

33   *Rainbow Babe in the Woods* (1979). Mixed media, collage on hankie, 9″ × 9¾″. Courtesy of Betye Saar.

34   *Baby* (1932). Crayon on paper, 8″ × 10″. Courtesy of Betye Saar.

35   *Black Girl's Window* (1969). Mixed media window, 35¾″ × 18″ × 1½″. Courtesy of Betye Saar.

36   *The Liberation of Aunt Jemima* (1972). Mixed media, 11¾″ × 2¾″. University Art Museum, University of California at Berkeley. Purchased with the aid of funds from the National Endowment for the Arts and selected by the Committee for the Acquisition of African-American Art. Photograph by Colin McRae.

37   *Record for Hattie* (1975). Assemblage box, 14″ × 13½″ × 2″. Courtesy of Betye Saar.

39   *Indigo Mercy* (detail) (1975). Mixed media, 42″ × 18½″ × 17″. In the collection of the Studio Museum in Harlem, New York. Courtesy of Betye Saar.

40   The Watts Towers. Photograph by Marvin Rand.

41   *Spirit Catcher* (1976–77). Mixed media floor assemblage, 3′ 9″ × 18″ × 18″. Courtesy of Betye Saar.

42   Betye Saar with *Mti* (1988). Photograph by Kenna Love. Taken from the book *Exposures: Women and Their Art,* photographs by Kenna Love, text by Betty Ann Brown and Arlene Raven (Pasadena, CA: New Sage Press, 1989).

43   Betye Saar and Alison Saar, *House of Gris Gris* (1990). Mixed media installation at the UCLA Wight Art Gallery, 1990, 7′ × 5′ × 6′. Photograph by Grey Crawford.

44   *Guardian of Desires* (1988). Free-standing assemblage, 10¾″ × 7¼″ × 2¾″. Courtesy of Betye Saar.

Mary Frank

46   Mary Frank at about age fourteen. Photograph. Courtesy of Mary Frank.

49   *Andrea and Pablo* (1962). Pen and ink, 5¼″ × 8¼″. Courtesy of Mary Frank.

51   *Journey* (1970). Ceramic, 21½″ × 22″. Courtesy of Mary Frank and Zabriskie Gallery, New York.

52   *Running Man/Walking Woman* (1981). Plaster and branches, 63½″ × 25½″ × 45″/65″ × 61″ × 57″. Courtesy of Mary Frank and Zabriskie Gallery, New York. Photograph by Ralph Gabriner.

53   Mary Frank in her New York City studio (1987 or 1988). Photograph by Joel Meyerowitz. Courtesy of Mary Frank.

53   *Woman* (1975). Ceramic, 22″ × 92″ × 28″. Collection of Richard Lippe. Courtesy of Mary Frank and Zabriskie Gallery, New York.

54   *Horse and Rider* (1982). Stoneware, 23½″ × 48″ × 28″. Everson Museum of Art, Syracuse, New York. Museum Purchase with Funds from the J. Stanley Coyne Foundation. Photograph by Courtney Frisse. P.C.83.8.

55,56   *Utterance* (full view and detail) (1984). Ceramic, 39½″ × 18″ × 26″. Private collection. Courtesy of Zabriskie Gallery, New York. Photograph by Ralph Gabriner.

57   *Self-Portrait* (1990). Charcoal drawing, 10½″ × 14¼″. Courtesy of Mary Frank.

58   *Dinosaur* (1980). Color monotype. Sheet and image: 24¾″ × 35½″ (62.9 cm. × 90.2 cm.). Collection of Whitney Museum of American Art, New York. Purchase, with funds from the Print Committee. 83.13.

59   *Flowers* (1991). Monoprint, 16″ × 20″. Courtesy of Mary Frank and Zabriskie Gallery, New York.

Bibliography

Heller, Nancy G. *Women Artists: An Illustrated History*. New York: Abbeville Press, 1987.

Munro, Eleanor. *Originals: American Women Artists*. New York: Simon & Schuster, 1979.

Rosen, Randy. *Making Their Mark: Women Artists Move into the Mainstream, 1970–85*. New York: Abbeville Press, 1989.

Rubenstein, Charlotte Streifer. *American Women Artists*. New York: Avon Books, 1982.

Mary Cassatt

Adato, Perry Miller. *Mary Cassatt—Impressionist from Philadelphia*. Videotape. WNET/Thirteen, New York City, 1975.

Breeskin, Adelyn D. *The Graphic Work of Mary Cassatt*. New York: H. Bittner, 1948.

Cain, Michael. *Mary Cassatt, Artist*. New York: Chelsea House, 1989.

Hale, Nancy. *Mary Cassatt*. (Radcliffe Biography Series.) Reading, MA: Addison-Wesley, 1987.

Lindsay, Suzanne G. *Mary Cassatt and Philadelphia,* exhibition catalogue. Philadelphia: Philadelphia Museum of Art, 1985.

McKown, Robin. *The World of Mary Cassatt*. New York: Dell, 1972.

Mary Cassatt—An American Observer, exhibition catalogue. New York: Coe Kerr Gallery, 1984.

Mathews, Nancy Mowll. *Mary Cassatt*. New York: Harry N. Abrams, 1987. In association with the National Museum of American Art, Smithsonian Institution.

———, ed. *Cassatt and Her Circle: Selected Letters*. New York: Abbeville Press, 1984.

———, and Barbara Stern Shapiro. *Mary Cassatt: The Color Prints*. New York: Harry N. Abrams, 1989. In association with Williams College Museum of Art, Williamstown, MA.

Meyer, Susan E. *Mary Cassatt*. New York: Harry N. Abrams, 1990.

Roudebush, Jay. *Mary Cassatt*. New York: Crown, 1979.

Segard, Achille. *Mary Cassatt: Un peintre des enfants et des mères*. Paris: Paul Ollendorff, 1913.

Leonora Carrington

Chadwick, Whitney. "Painting on the Threshold," essay in *Leonora Carrington,* exhibition catalogue. New York: Brewster Gallery, 1988.

———. *Women Artists and the Surrealist Movement*. Boston: Little, Brown, 1985.

Grimberg, Salomón. Conversations about Leonora Carrington, 1991–92.

Kaplan, Janet A. *Unexpected Journeys: The Art and Life of Remedios Varo*. New York: Abbeville Press, 1988.

Leonora Carrington: The Mexican Years, 1943–1985, exhibition catalogue. San Francisco: The Mexican Museum, 1991.

Orenstein, Gloria Feman. "Leonora Carrington: Another Reality." *Ms,* August 1974, pp. 27–31.

———. "Leonora Carrington's Visionary Art for the New Age." *Chrysalis* 3 (1977), pp. 66–77.

———. "Women of Surrealism." In *Feminist Collage,* ed. Judy Loeb. New York: Teachers College Press, 1979.

Schlieker, Andrea, ed. *Leonora Carrington,* exhibition catalogue. London: Serpentine Gallery, 1991.

Betye Saar

Campbell, Mary Schmidt. *Rituals: The Art of Betye Saar,* exhibition catalogue. New York: The Studio Museum of Harlem, 1980.

Clothier, Peter. "The Other Side of the Past," essay in *Betye Saar,* exhibition catalogue. Los Angeles: The Museum of Contemporary Art, 1984.

Glueck, Grace. "Betye Saar, Artist Inspired by Occult." *New York Times,* February 16, 1978.

Hopkins, Henry, and Mimi Jacobs. *Fifty West Coast Artists.* San Francisco: Chronicle Books, 1981.

Lippard, Lucy. *Mixed Blessings.* New York: Pantheon, 1990.

Love, Kenna, photographer. *Exposures: Women and Their Art.* Text by Betty Ann Brown and Arlene Raven. Pasadena, CA: New Sage Press, 1989.

Shepherd, Elizabeth, ed. *The Art of Betye and Alison Saar: Secrets, Dialogues, Revelations,* exhibition catalogue. Los Angeles: Wight Art Gallery, UCLA, 1990.

Sills, Leslie. Conversation with Betye Saar. New York City, May 11, 1990.

Sims, Lowery S. "Betye Saar," essay in Women's Caucus for Art Honor Awards Catalogue. San Francisco: National Women's Caucus for Art Conference, 1989.

Mary Frank

Herrera, Hayden. *Mary Frank.* New York: Harry N. Abrams, 1990.

———. *Mary Frank: Sculpture, Drawings, Prints,* Neuberger Museum exhibition catalogue. Purchase, N.Y.: State University of New York, 1978.

Hughes, Robert. "Images of Metamorphosis." *Time,* July 10, 1978.

Mary Frank: Sculpture, Prints, and Drawings, exhibition catalogue. Lincoln, MA: DeCordova and Dana Museum and Park, 1988.

Matthiessen, Peter, and Mary Frank. *Shadows of Africa.* New York: Harry N. Abrams, 1992.

Moorman, Margaret. "In a Timeless World." *ArtNews,* May 1987, pp. 90–98.

Raynor, Vivien. "Art: One Woman Shows at the Brooklyn Museum." *New York Times,* March 27, 1987.

Sawin, Martica. "The Sculpture of Mary Frank." *Arts,* March 1977.

Sills, Leslie. Conversation with Mary Frank. New York City, January 16, 1991.

Tarlow, Lois. "Mary Frank: Profile." *Art New England,* February 1988, pp. 6–7.

Leslie Sills earned a degree in psychology from Boston University. After graduation, she pursued a strong interest in art, studying ceramic sculpture at the School of the Museum of Fine Arts in Boston. She also taught art classes to children in her home.

Through teaching, she discovered a serious lack of information about women artists. Her desire to remedy this situation led to her first book, *Inspirations: Stories About Women Artists,* as well as to many talks to schoolchildren about women artists.

Leslie Sills' own artwork explores issues of birth, death, and sexuality from a female point of view. Her recent sculptures are primitive figures made of clay, wood, and papier mâché. "Making art has been an essential part of my life since I was twenty-one," she says. She hopes that her art will help women to feel recognized and celebrated.

Ms. Sills continues to teach small art classes in Brookline, Massachusetts. One of her favorite classes consists of six boys, including her six-year-old son, Eric.